THIS WALKER BOOK BELONGS TO:

_____

_____

_____

_____

First published as *This Is the Bear* (1986)
and *This Is the Bear and the Scary Night* (1991)
by Walker Books Ltd
87 Vauxhall Walk, London SE11 5HJ

This edition published 1998

2 4 6 8 10 9 7 5 3 1

This book has been typeset in Bembo.

Printed in Hong Kong

British Library Cataloguing in Publication Data
A catalogue record for this book is available
from the British Library.

ISBN 0-7445-6702-5 (hb)
ISBN 0-7445-6380-1 (pb)

THIS IS THE
BEAR

—————— *and* ——————

THIS IS THE
BEAR
AND THE SCARY NIGHT

WRITTEN BY
Sarah Hayes

ILLUSTRATED BY
Helen Craig

WALKER BOOKS
AND SUBSIDIARIES

LONDON • BOSTON • SYDNEY

For Barbara, who makes bears
S.H.

For Edward (Teddy) Craig
H.C.

THIS IS THE
BEAR

This is the bear
who fell in the bin.

This is the dog
who pushed him in.

This is the man
who picked up the sack.

This is the driver
who would not come back.

This is the bear
who went to the dump

and fell on the pile
with a bit of a bump.

This is the boy

who took the bus

and went to the dump
to make a fuss.

This is the man
in an awful grump
who searched

and searched
and searched the dump.

This is the bear
all cold and cross

who did not think
he was really lost.

This is the dog
who smelled the smell

of a bone

and a tin

and a bear as well.

This is the man
who drove them home –

the boy, the bear
and the dog with a bone.

This is the bear
all lovely and clean

who did not say
just where he had been.

This is the boy
who knew quite well,

but promised his friend
he would not tell.

And this is the boy
who woke up in the night
and asked the bear
if he felt all right –
and was very surprised
when the bear shouted out,
'How soon can we have
another day out?'

For Amelia
with our love.
S.H. & H.C.

THIS IS THE
BEAR
AND THE SCARY NIGHT

This is the boy
who forgot his bear

and left him behind
in the park on a chair.

This is the bear
who looked at the moon

and hoped the boy
would come back soon.

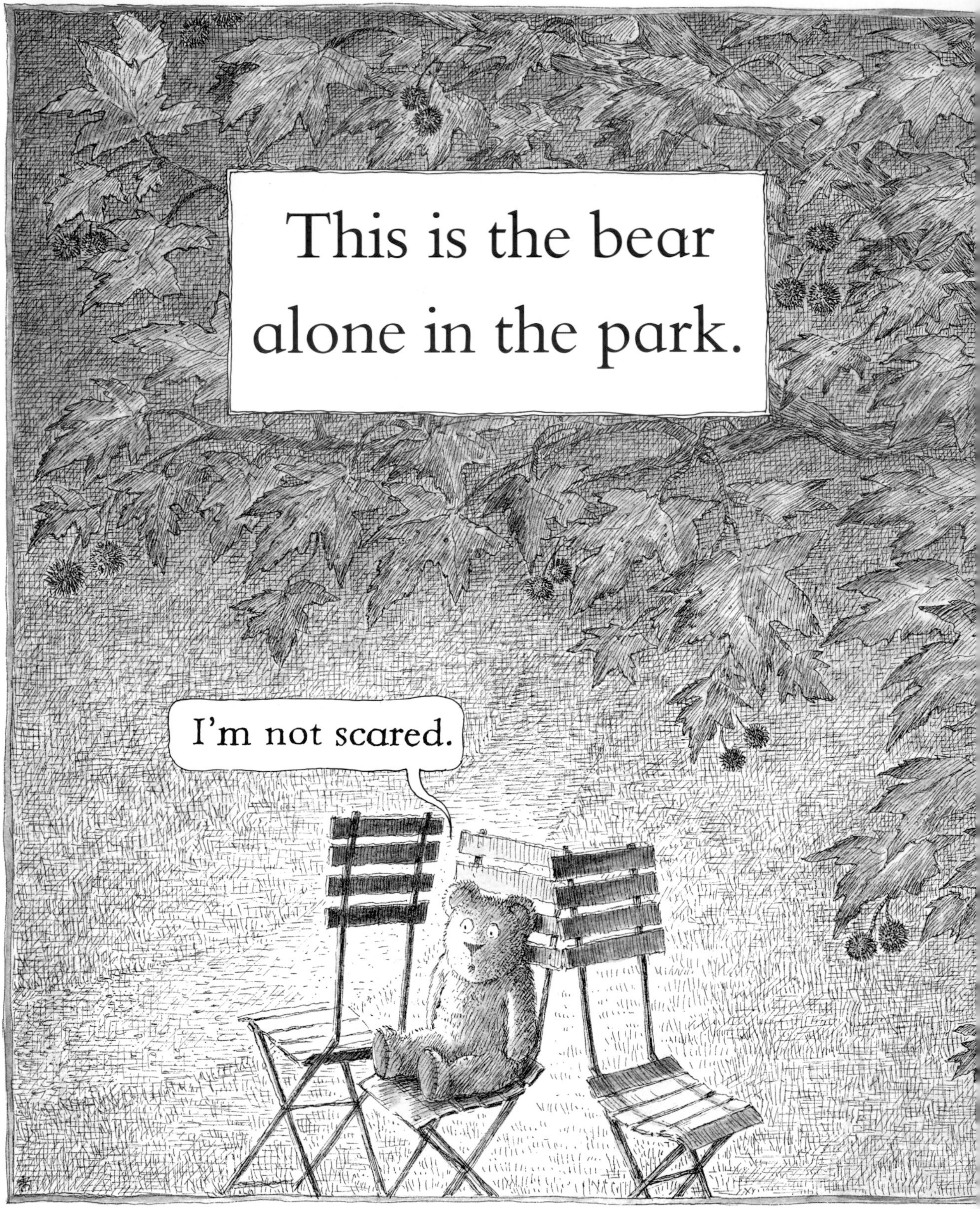
This is the bear
alone in the park.
I'm not scared.

These are the eyes
which glowed in the dark.

WHOOOOOOOOOOOOO!

This is the owl
who swooped in the night
and gave the bear
a terrible fright.

This is the bear
up in the sky.
This is the owl
who struggled to fly.

Oh no!

These are the claws
which couldn't hold on.
And this is the bear
who fell ...

This is the bear
who floated all night.

This is the dark
which turned into light.

This is the man
with the slide trombone

who rescued the bear
and took him home.

This is the bear
in a warm blue sweater
who made a friend
and felt much better.

This is the boy
who remembered his bear

and ran to the park
and found him there.

This is the bear
who started to tell

how he flew through the air
and how he fell ...

and how he floated
and how he was saved
and how he was
terribly terribly brave.
And this is the boy
who grinned and said,
'I know a bear
who is ready for bed.'

MORE WALKER PAPERBACKS
For You to Enjoy

Also by Sarah Hayes and Helen Craig

THIS IS THE BEAR AND THE PICNIC LUNCH

The boy packs a picnic lunch, the bear guards it and the dog steals it!

"Delightful." *Wendy Cope, The Daily Telegraph*

0-7445-1304-9   £4.99

THIS IS THE BEAR AND THE BAD LITTLE GIRL

The boy and the dog have to move fast to save their friend the bear
when a bad little girl runs off with him!

"Rhyme is very important to toddlers in the process of learning to read.
This adventure story told in rhyme is sure to capture their imaginations."
Mother & Baby

0-7445-4771-7   £4.99

MARY MARY

Included on the list of texts to be used in conjunction with the
Standard Assessment Tasks of the National Curriculum (Key Stage 2, Level 1 – 2).

"Giants are always popular with children and this fairy tale has a
friendly giant and an intrepid heroine, two excellent ingredients for a winning story."
Child Education

0-7445-2062-2   £4.99